My Two Grannies

Floella Benjamin

Illustrated by Margaret Chamberlain

F

FRANCES LINCOLN
CHILDREN'S BOOKS

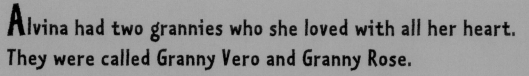

Alvina had two grannies who she loved with all her heart.
They were called Granny Vero and Granny Rose.
   Granny Vero was born on the Caribbean island of Trinidad
and Granny Rose was born in the Yorkshire town of Barnsley.
Now they both lived in the same city as Alvina and her parents.

"Tell me about Trinidad again," Alvina begged.
   "Don't you ever get tired of hearing
the same stories, Alvina?" said Granny Vero.
   "Never!" said Alvina.
   "When I was your age we would go to the beach,
and splash around in the tropical sea," said
Granny Vero, with a big smile on her face.
"We never wanted to come out of that warm water."

"I would love to do that, Granny V," said Alvina.
"Well, one day I will take you to Trinidad, darlin',"
said Granny Vero. "I promise."

When Alvina saw Granny Rose, she asked,
"Did you swim in the sea all day when you were little?"

"No, luvvie," laughed Granny Rose. "The sea
in Blackpool was much too cold.
But we did play on the
beach all day long and
ride on the donkeys.
We must all go to
Blackpool one day so you
can do that too."

"Oh, yes please!"
said Alvina.

Both grannies loved to play music on their old
record players and Alvina loved listening to it.
Granny Rose played brass band music.

"This music always reminds me of
when we used to go to the park
on Sundays to listen to the local
brass band. On May Day we would
watch the morris dancers fling
their arms in the air and jingle
the bells on their legs as they
twirled around the maypole
to the music."

"Let's try it, Granny R," said Alvina, and they both
fell exhausted into a heap of laughter when they tried
to do the morris dance.

Granny Vero's favourite music was Calypso and steelpan.

"This is what they used to play in Trinidad," Granny Vero explained to Alvina. "It always made me want to dance in the streets at carnival time. Come on Alvina, shake your waist while you dance."

"Like this, Granny V?"
"That's right, darlin'."

One day Alvina's two grannies were at her house for tea. Alvina's mum said, "It will be our tenth wedding anniversary next month."

"Why don't the two of you go away together? I'll be more than happy to look after Alvina," said Granny Vero.

"No, I will look after her. She can come and stay with me," said Granny Rose.

The two grannies argued and argued about who would look after Alvina. So Alvina said, "Why don't you both stay here and look after me!"

The two grannies frowned at each other but agreed. Yes, they would both look after Alvina.

The day arrived when Alvina's parents were going off on holiday.

"Have a nice time," said Alvina hugging her mum and dad tightly.

"We are going to miss you," said Mum.

"Be a good girl for your grannies," said Dad.

"I will," said Alvina.

"Don't worry, I will look after her," said Granny Vero.
"And so will I," said Granny Rose.

At bedtime the two grannies both wanted
to tell Alvina a story.
"How about an Anansi story?" said Granny Vero.
"Or I could tell you the story of
Jack and the Beanstalk," said Granny Rose.

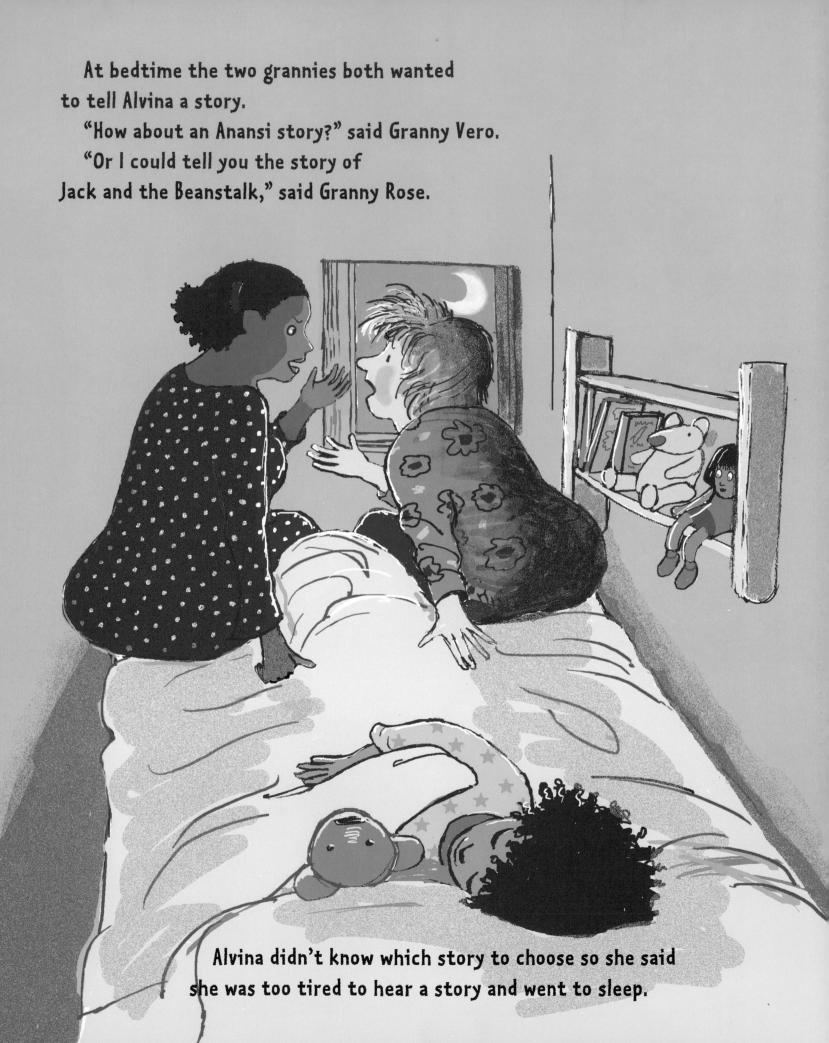

Alvina didn't know which story to choose so she said
she was too tired to hear a story and went to sleep.

The next morning when Alvina got up she had an idea. She sat down with the two grannies at the breakfast table.

"Granny V and Granny R, I love the things you both do for me so why don't you take turns. Granny V can do everything one day and Granny R can do everything the next day!"

And that's what happened.

They all played dominoes the way Granny Vero did when she was a girl. Afterwards Granny Vero cooked peas and rice, chicken and plantains with mango flan for pudding.

"This is lovely, Granny V," said Alvina tucking in.

"Mmmm, very nice," said Granny Rose. "You must give me the recipe."

They went to the zoo and saw the agouti and the toucan – the animals Granny Vero had seen in the forest as a girl in Trinidad.

"It must have been wonderful to see those animals in the wild," said Granny Rose.

That night Granny Vero told an exciting Anansi story.
"Anansi would turn himself into a spider whenever
he was in trouble," she said.

"Or if he wanted to play a trick," chipped in Alvina,
who couldn't help joining in.

"That Anansi sounds crafty," said Granny Rose.

"He is," said Alvina, with eyes wide as saucers.

Alvina gave both her grannies a big hug and fell fast asleep
with a smile on her face. The grannies smiled too.

The next day it was Granny Rose's turn. They played snakes and ladders.
"Down the snake I go," said Granny Rose.
"Never mind, Granny R," said Alvina. "You won the last game."
Then they went to the park and Alvina fed the ducks.
"That duck is greedy. It's eating all the bread," laughed Alvina.
"I'll give them some too," said Granny Vero. "This is fun."

Granny Rose cooked steak and kidney pie
with mashed potatoes and carrots and apple pie
for pudding.

"You must show me how to make steak and kidney pie,"
said Granny Vero. "It's delicious."

At bedtime Granny Rose told the story of Jack and the Beanstalk.

"Fee fi fo fum, I smell the blood of an Englishman…"
Alvina and Granny Rose said together.

"I like that part of the story," Alvina said.
"Run Jack, run!"

"Yes, run Jack!" giggled Granny Vero.

Fee fi fo

fum

The two grannies took turns for the rest of the week to look after Alvina. They really got to know each other better.

When Alvina's parents came back from holiday
she was excited to see them.

"Did you have a nice time with your grannies?"
asked Mum.

"Oh yes," said Alvina. "We had lots of fun.
They both made me feel so special."

"That's because we love you," chirped the two grannies and they gave her a **great big hug.**

My Two Grannies copyright © Frances Lincoln Limited 2007
Text copyright © Floella Benjamin 2007
Illustrations copyright © Margaret Chamberlain 2007

First published in Great Britain in 2007 and in the USA in 2008 by
Frances Lincoln Children's Books, 4 Torriano Mews,
Torriano Avenue, London NW5 2RZ

www.franceslincoln.com

British Library Cataloguing in Publication Data available on request

ISBN: 978-1-84507-643-6

Printed in China

1 3 5 7 9 8 6 4 2